Frog Medicine

by MARK TEAGUE

SCHOLASTIC INC.
New York Toronto London Auckland Sydney

Elmo Freem wasn't paying attention
the morning Mrs. Drindle brought
in books for book reports.
In fact, he was so busy watching a strange insect
crawl across his desk that he failed to notice
his classmates going to choose their books.
By the time he realized what was happening,
it was too late.
The only book left was a small, shabby, greenish
thing with an odd title. Elmo groaned when he read it.
FROG MEDICINE, read the cover,
BY DOCTOR FRANK GALOOF.

That afternoon Elmo tried trading the book
for something better, but the other kids just laughed.
"Frog Medicine!" they shouted.
"Who cares about that?"

Secretly Elmo agreed. Frogs were
dull creatures, in his opinion, good only
for eating bugs and sitting in puddles.
How interesting could the book be?
When he got home he threw it into his closet
without even looking at it.
"I'll read it later," he told his cat, Leon.

The week passed and things got worse.
The longer Elmo put off the project,
the harder it seemed.

Everyone else was enjoying the assignment.
Roy Plumpton was reading a book called
Common Household Monsters, and Arthur Flux
had already finished his report on
The Lost Dinosaurs of Terror Island.
Even Buford Snark, who rarely did schoolwork
at all, was clearly enjoying *Space Aliens and You.*
It all seemed very unfair.

Elmo tried to think about other,
more pleasant subjects,
but his thoughts kept drifting back to
the book in his closet. At the same time it seemed
as though there were frogs everywhere he looked.
"I wish they would all just go away," he thought.

The night before the report was due
Elmo began to panic. He took out paper and a pencil
and sat down at the desk in his bedroom.
"I haven't got time to read the book," he told Leon.
"I'll just make up something."

But try as he might, he could think of nothing
to say. He fell asleep still worrying.

The next morning was dark and rainy.

Elmo felt sick.

"I can't go to school," he told his mother.

She looked at him closely and felt his forehead.

"Maybe a nice, hot bath would help," she said.

"Get into the tub, and I'll run to the store

for some medicine."

In the bathtub Elmo made a terrible discovery.

His feet had grown long, slimy, and green.

There were webs between his toes. "Oh, no!" he cried,

"I'm turning into a frog!"

Just then he remembered the book.

"Frog Medicine! That's what I need."

And he hopped out of the tub to get it.

He didn't even need to open the book
to find what he wanted. Doctor Galoof's
phone number was printed on the back cover.
"He'll know what to do," said Elmo
as he hopped to the phone.

The doctor answered on the first ring, and
he listened patiently as Elmo explained his problem.

"Ah! That's very rare," he said.
His voice was deep and gravelly. "Wait outside.
I'll send a cab to bring you to my office."

A few minutes later Elmo and Leon
were standing on the sidewalk in front
of their apartment building. It was raining heavily.
Great waterfalls fell from the rooftops,
and the streets ran like rivers. Leon, who didn't
like the rain much, hid under Elmo's shirt.

The cab that came to pick them up was
unlike any Elmo had seen before. It was covered
with patches of deep, green moss, and when it moved
it made a loud, wet, croaking sound. The driver
was equally strange. Although he wore a tall hat,
he was so short that they could barely see
him over the top of the seat. He sang an odd,
burping song as he drove, though Elmo wasn't quite
able to make out the words. Still he was very nice,
and he told them both to make themselves comfortable.

With all the wet weather the cab seemed
to float along, rushing down side streets
until Elmo was lost.

At some point he became certain that
they really were floating. The rain slowed, and
the streets became like quiet ponds. Enormous lily pads
floated on the surface. The buildings, although still
very tall, were wet and mossy, and many were hung
with vines. A sign read WELCOME TO FROGTOWN.

"Imagine that," said Elmo.

Doctor Galoof's office was at the end
of the street (or pond, Elmo couldn't decide which)
and it was partly underwater. Elmo thanked
the driver as they got out. He waded to
the front door with Leon perched on his shoulder.
"What a strange place," he said.

Even so, they were both surprised
by the appearance of Dr. Galoof. Although he wore
a lab coat and a stethoscope, the doctor
was clearly a frog.

"Welcome," he said cheerfully.
"And what seems to be the problem?"

Elmo didn't know quite where to begin,
so he told the doctor about his trouble with school
and about the book report he had been unable to write.

"Ah, yes," said the doctor as he pulled the book
from his shelf. "*Frog Medicine*. A wonderful book,
if I do say so myself. How did you like it?"

Elmo was very embarrassed. He told the doctor
how he'd been meaning to read the book, but that
he'd kept putting it off until it was too late.

Doctor Galoof smiled.

"Well, there's your problem," he said.

"Go home and read. Then write your report."

"But you don't understand," said Elmo, and he lifted his foot out of the water.

"I'm turning into a frog."

"It's no surprise," said the doctor.

"You see, the longer you put a problem off, the worse it becomes. It's all in my book."

Elmo was not convinced.

"I thought you might have some medicine —" he began.

Doctor Galoof shook his head.

"Just do your homework.

The rest should take care of itself."

Since it was nearly lunchtime,
the doctor took them out to eat. The restaurant
was colorful, in a swampy sort of way, and although
the food was not very appetizing to Elmo,
Leon didn't seem to mind. Dr. Galoof
was a pleasant host. With Leon he discussed
the art of catching flies, and he told them both
a great deal about Frogtown.

"I had no idea frogs led such
interesting lives," said Elmo.

"You really should read more,"
said the doctor.

After lunch Dr. Galoof put them back
into the cab. "You shouldn't be late
getting home," he said.
"Time moves pretty slowly here in Frogtown."
Then he gave them both slimy hugs
and sent them on their way.

"Read the book!" he shouted
to Elmo as they pulled away.
"I think you'll enjoy it."

Elmo did enjoy the book. He opened it up
as soon as they got home, and found that it was
full of interesting facts and strange pictures.
As he read he began to feel better. By the time
he finished reading, his worries were gone,
and his feet had returned to normal.

When his mother came back from the store
she was happy to see him feeling so good.
She put the medicine away and smiled.
"You should be well enough for school
tomorrow," she said.

Standing at his window, Elmo looked out
over the city. The storm had blown away, and
the streets were drying under a warm afternoon sun.
Leon lay on the windowsill.
Elmo smiled and sat down to write his report.

For John

The artwork in this book
was painted in acrylics.

ISBN 0-590-44178-7

Copyright © 1991 by Mark Teague.
All rights reserved. Published by Scholastic Inc.
BLUE RIBBON is a registered trademark of Scholastic Inc.

12 11 10 9 8 7 6 5 4 3 2 1   3 4 5 6 7/9

Printed in the U.S.A.   08